THE LOST
WORLD

KRESTOR
THE CRUSHING
TERROR

With special thanks to J.N. Richards

For Sam's boys Taylor, Dion and Amari

www.beastquest.co.uk

ORCHARD BOOKS
338 Euston Road, London NW1 3BH
Orchard Books Australia
Level 17/207 Kent St, Sydney, NSW 2000

A Paperback Original
First published in Great Britain in 2010

Beast Quest is a registered trademark of Beast Quest Limited
Series created by Working Partners Limited, London

Text © Beast Quest Limited 2010
Cover and inside illustrations by Steve Sims © Orchard Books 2010

A CIP catalogue record for this book is available from
the British Library.

ISBN 978 1 40830 731 1

5 7 9 10 8 6

Printed and bound by CPI Group (UK) Ltd, Croydon, CR0 4YY

The paper and board used in this paperback are natural recyclable
products made from wood grown in sustainable forests. The
manufacturing processes conform to the environmental regulations of
the country of origin.

Orchard Books is a division of Hachette Children's Books,
an Hachette UK company

www.hachette.co.uk

KRESTOR
THE CRUSHING
TERROR

BY ADAM BLADE

ORCHARD BOOKS

THE FOREST
OF DOOM

SOUTHERN RIVER

THE
SCARLET
DESERT

Welcome to another world, where Dark Forces are at play.

Tom thought he was on his way back home; he was wrong. My son has entered another realm where nothing is as it seems. Six monstrous Beasts threaten all corners of the kingdom, and Tom and Elenna must face an enemy they thought long gone. I have never been so proud of my son, but can he be all that I always hoped he would be? Or shall a mother watch her son fail?

One question remains. Are you brave enough to join Tom on the most deadly Quest yet?

Only you know the answer...

Freya, Mistress of the Beasts

PROLOGUE

Aquillus spread his wings as a swell
of warm air lifted him higher.

He soared over a mountain range,
but tiredness flooded through him.
He'd been hunting for far longer than
he wanted and still had no food to
show for it. He thought of his chicks,
their beaks open with hunger. They
would starve if he did not feed them
soon. Aquillus couldn't go on like
this. He needed rest.

The eagle spotted a sun-bleached

tree, clinging to the mountainside where he could rest. He swooped downwards.

Aquillus landed on the uppermost branch of the tree and folded his wings. Tavania's mountains reared up in front of him, unforgiving and proud. The small streams that used to flow between white rocks were dry.

The branch beneath Aquillus shuddered in a stiff breeze. The eagle clung on with his yellow talons, then opened his wings and slowly rose into the air. He may not have been able to find water, but maybe he could find food. An unwary mountain rodent, perhaps, out searching for something to drink...

His sharp eyes searched the mountains but he saw no creatures darting between the rocky crevices.

Aquillus could almost hear the urgent squawk of his chicks. He'd left them for too long. Failure seemed to weigh him down as he angled himself in the direction of his nest.

A glimmer of something between the rocks caught his eye. A small pool of water! A new wave of energy surged through the eagle and he hurtled downwards. He landed nimbly, sending up a spray of small stones. Eagerly, he dipped his beak into the pool.

Pain!

Fire blazed through Aquillus's beak. Liquid fire scorched his throat and his eyes rolled back as agony swamped him. The pool wasn't water – it was some kind of acid!

The eagle opened his wings to fly away but his mind was fogged with panic. Aquillus's talons skittered on the gravel and he veered to the side, one magnificent wing dipping into the pool of deadly liquid. Pain raged up his wing and Aquillus smelt his feathers burning. He fell back from the acid but didn't dare look at his wing. He could guess what he'd find – a charred, bloody tangle of feathers and bone. Would he ever be able to fly again?

The eagle's vision blurred but he made out the shape of something moving. Aquillus blinked. An enormous Beast was winding its way through the rocks. Its broad back was covered with sharp spines that glinted in the low light. Its neck was long and serpent-like, and its head was green and misshapen. A forked tongue flickered out of its mouth.

This Beast was a sea creature! What's it doing in the mountains? It looked at Aquillus with an evil glint in its eye, readying itself to attack.

The eagle tried to heave his broken body away but his enemy was faster, despite its webbed claws.

Desperately, Aquillus beat his healthy wing, but it was not enough to take him up into the sky. The Beast's long neck snaked out towards him. Up close, the eagle could see the Beast's face with its two bulging red eyes, a bulbous snout and wide mouth. His jaws were lined with long, pointed teeth. The Beast let out a growl, and saliva dripped from its needle-sharp teeth.

Aquillus just managed to drag himself out of reach as the Beast's jaws snapped shut behind him.

There was a tremor beneath
Aquillus's talons and the eagle turned
to see that the Beast was using its
head as a club, beating the ground
with it's huge lower jaw, causing

cracks to open in the rocks.

Aquillus staggered, vainly trying to keep his balance. The Beast struck out, wrapping its long neck around him. Frantically, Aquillus slashed with his talons and beak, tearing into his enemy's thick skin. The Beast gave a roar of pain and loosened his grip.

The eagle took his chance and heaved himself free, only to find that he was right on the edge of a mountain ledge. His talons slipped off the edge in a shower of sparks. He couldn't fly! He saw the parched ground far below and felt his body tip forwards. He fell through the air, feeling cold eddies circling him.

My young, who will feed my young? Aquillus plunged into the abyss…

CHAPTER ONE

A PRICKLY ISSUE

"Elenna, it looks really bad," Tom
said anxiously, staring at the burn
mark on Storm's flank and seeing
that the edges were badly inflamed.
Storm gave a small whinny of
discomfort, and Silver, the wolf,
rubbed his shaggy head against the
stallion's leg.

"Don't worry, I have the perfect
thing to treat it." Elenna reached into

her quiver of arrows and took out a pouch, which contained her healing herbs. "I'll make a poultice, but I'll need you to get me some water."

Tom grabbed the flask from Storm's saddlebag and ran to the small stream that wound out from the Forest of Doom.

As he filled the flask, Tom peered between the trees. He'd faced Hellion the Fiery Foe in the gloom of the forest. Hellion had been a fearsome opponent with limbs of fire and molten muscles. Tom and his friends had almost died trying to defeat the Beast, and poor Storm had got burnt during the fight.

Tom headed back to his faithful stallion. Pride rose in him as he looked at the brave horse. Together, he, Elenna, Storm and Silver had triumphed, and Hellion had been sent back to his part of the kingdom through one of the portals that scored the sky of Tavania.

But my Quest is not over yet, Tom reminded himself. The Dark Wizard, Malvel, still sat on Tavania's throne, and Tom had to defeat four other Beasts and return them to their proper homes.

Tom handed Elenna the flask of water and she quickly mixed up a thick poultice, which she slathered onto Storm's wound.

"There, that should take away the pain. It will be healed in no time," Elenna said, wiping her hands on a scrap of cloth.

Tom stroked Storm's mane and grinned at Elenna. "What would we do without you and your herbs?"

Elenna laughed. "Don't be too hard
on yourself, Tom, you have your
uses. To start with, you're really good
at reading maps!"

Tom took his golden map from
Storm's saddlebag, unfolding the
hinged squares to reveal an etched
landscape of Tavania. He could see
the Forest of Doom and the area of

scrubland that stretched out in front of them. Tom held his breath as a path of glowing amber snaked through the scrubland and towards a tiny image of a castle.

Tom squinted into the distance. There, on the horizon, he could see the stark shape of the fortress.

Elenna followed his gaze. "Isn't that Cordwell castle?" she asked.

"Yes, I think so. Back in Avantia it was just a ruin," Tom replied. "Here in Tavania it still stands." Tavania had many of the same landmarks as Tom's own kingdom, though there was always something slightly different about each one.

"It's so strange," Elenna said softly. "Seeing familiar places like this makes me feel almost at home. But we're not."

"I bet we can guess what lies behind that castle," Tom said.

"The Northern Mountains," Elenna replied.

"Known here as the Northern Peaks." Tom pointed to the trail on the map, which stretched past the castle and stopped at a portal nestled between dusty mountaintops. Below the drawing were the words, 'The Northern Peaks'.

Tom felt a rush of excitement at the adventure that lay ahead. The wizard, Oradu, had already told them that they'd be facing a new Beast called Krestor. "We need to get on with our Quest. Let's go!"

Tom and Elenna mounted Storm and rode across the scrubland, with Silver running alongside. Suddenly the wolf gave a yelp. Tom looked down to see that prickly thistles had snagged on Silver's fur and were caught in his silvery pelt. Looking over his shoulder, Tom spotted several more thistles caught in Storm's tail and haunches.

"Elenna, we need to stop." He drew Storm to a halt. Jumping out of his saddle he pointed to a large thistle

that was pressed into Silver's side.

Elenna gasped and climbed down. "These thistles are alive!" she exclaimed. "Look at the barbs on them, they're wriggling!"

Tom reached out and plucked off a pulsing thistle. The barbs on it quivered in excitement and scratched his hand. Tom gave a growl of annoyance and dropped the prickly weed before stamping on it. "These thistles have been enchanted," Tom guessed. "It's all part of the Dark Wizard's magic." He shook his head in disgust. "Even nature has turned evil with Malvel sitting on Tavania's throne. Elenna, if you mount Storm and keep him calm, I'll pick off the rest of these thistles."

Tom made short work of removing the barbed weeds from Storm and

Silver's bodies. He sucked at a bloody scratch on his palm. "All done, come on, we should get go—"

A tremor ripped through the ground. Tom crouched low to keep his balance as the vibrations travelled up his legs. The ground juddered again and Elenna yelled as Storm reared up in distress. His friend was thrown from Storm's back, flipping through the air.

"Elenna!" Tom cried. Her body hit the earth. The ground beneath Tom's feet rumbled as he ran over to her, Silver close at his heels. Elenna groaned as Tom helped her up.

"Just a few scrapes," she reassured him. "What's happening?"

"It's an earthquake," Tom said as cracks blossomed across the earth. "And we're in the middle of it!"

CHAPTER TWO

TERROR TREMOR

The ground gave another shudder as an even bigger tremor ripped through the earth.

"Come on, we've got to get out of here. It's not safe!" Tom shouted over Storm's panicked neighs and Silver's howls. He looked down as yet more cracks appeared in the scrubby ground.

The two friends leapt into Storm's

saddle, and the stallion hurtled across the juddering ground. Tom and Elenna stayed low against Storm's back, urging him on as more tremors struck. Tom could see a blur by his side. It was Silver, his ears flat against his head as he raced beside them.

Other creatures were fleeing the earthquake, too. Rabbits, deer and foxes crashed out of the undergrowth and charged alongside Silver.

"Stop!" Elenna screamed, pointing to a crack racing across the ground towards them.

Tom yanked on Storm's reins, just as the ground in front of the stallion's hooves split open with a grinding sound. Fear mounted inside him. The crevice looked just like a huge set of jaws with spikes of rock for teeth! *This is definitely Malvel's dark magic,*

Tom thought angrily.

Storm skittered backwards, but a rabbit by his side was not as quick. For a moment the floppy-eared creature clung to the crevice's edge, but then slid, squealing with terror, into the dark chasm. The crevice snapped shut over the animal. With an ominous rumble the crack started racing across the ground towards Storm.

"Tom, what are we going to do?" Elenna cried from behind him. "It's going to swallow us!"

Tom snapped Storm's reins. "Go on, boy," he urged, digging his heels into the horse's side. The stallion leapt into a gallop, veering to the right and pulling away from the crevice. Silver sprinted along with them, crossing the shaking scrubland.

Tom turned in his saddle. The crevice had opened up even wider and was racing after them, huge chunks of earth falling into the void. Storm gave a whinny of fear as he tripped on a loose rock and reared up.

"Hold on to me!" Tom called, grabbing Elenna and taking the full brunt of the fall as they were thrown from Storm's back. Staggering to their feet, Tom saw that the crevice had caught up with them. Storm's rear hooves were about to slip over the edge. He was going to topple into the chasm!

"Storm, no!" Tom cried, as he scrambled over to his horse.

Elenna ran by his side and together they grabbed Storm's bridle. "Pull him back up!" she shouted, wrapping

the leather of the harness around her
hand. Silver snarled at the chasm, his
hackles standing on end.

"Pull!" Tom yelled. The ground
beneath them shuddered again and
more chunks of earth fell into the

waiting abyss. He just hoped the ground beneath his feet would hold long enough to save Storm.

Storm scrabbled with his hind legs over the ridge, his hooves smashing against its rocky edge. The stallion thrashed his head from side to side, the whites of his eyes showing.

"Storm, hang on," Tom begged. He could feel the bridle slipping from his hands as sweat sprung up on his palms.

Gritting his teeth, he held on more tightly, even as the leather of the bridle cut into his flesh. The muscles in his arms felt like they were on fire, and beside him Elenna gave a sob.

"Tom, I don't think I can hold on much long—" Her words stopped abruptly as she let out a scream of pain and dropped the bridle.

Tom looked over and saw that his friend's hands had been badly cut by the leather harness, and her fingers were clenched like claws.

"I'm sorry," Elenna cried. "M-my hands!"

Tom let out a grunt of pain as he tried to hold Storm's weight by himself. The stallion reared and clambered, but the edge of the crevice crumbled away with each strike of his hooves. Storm couldn't hold himself up! Tom's arms were being pulled from their sockets, the sinews straining. "Elenna, I can't hold him by myself, he—" Tom broke off, his eyes meeting Storm's frightened gaze as the stallion tipped back even further. "He's going to fall…"

With a scream of terror, Storm plunged downwards.

CHAPTER THREE

SILVER'S COURAGE

Silver leapt through the air. His jaws snapped around Storm's bridle, helping Tom to hold the stallion up.

Tom felt strength course through his arms. *While there's blood in my veins I will not lose Storm*, he vowed to himself. *I will not let Malvel win*. He dug his heels into the earth and leant back, blinking the sweat out of his eyes. With a final growl of effort, he and Silver hauled Storm out of the chasm's reach.

For a moment, the crevice opened even wider. Then, before their eyes, it snapped shut, sending up clouds of dust. There were muffled groans and creaks beneath their feet and then everything was still.

"Is it gone?" Elenna said shakily.

Tom nodded. "It looks like Malvel's magic can only last so long."

Elenna threw herself at Storm and wrapped her arms around his neck. "I'm so sorry I let you down," she murmured into the horse's glossy coat.

Tom put a hand on Elenna's shoulder. "What are you talking about? You helped." He knelt and ruffled Silver's fur. "You both did."

Elenna and Tom quickly examined the stallion for any sign of injury. Tom gingerly stroked a hand down Storm's back legs and the horse let out a snort of pain. He looked more closely and saw that one of the legs was swollen round the ankle. Storm seemed reluctant to rest any weight on the injured leg.

"I'm going to make a compress,"

Elenna said. "That should take the swelling down." She pulled a cooking pot out of the saddlebag and threw some of her herbs into it. Adding more water from the flask, she stirred the mixture well. Tom ripped a spare linen tunic into strips, and with a nod from Elenna, dipped the lengths of fabric into the liquid.

Gently, Elenna bound Storm's ankle, holding the strips of linen tight and fastening them.

"There, there," she murmured to the horse. Storm bowed his head and blew gratefully into her hair. Elenna laughed. "Stop it, Storm! It tickles!"

Tom looked up at the darkening sky. The stars reflected off the glassy dome that encased all of Tavania. In the distance, past the castle, he could see the portal hanging over the mountaintops. Eerie lights burst and flickered around the portal's edge like one of Aduro's magical firework displays. Homesickness slammed into him, but he stiffened his resolve. *Somewhere a Beast is waiting for me*, he told himself. *I have a Quest to complete.*

"We should stay here until morning before travelling any further," Tom said. "We need some sleep."

Elenna nodded. "A rest will do Storm good, and hopefully his leg will heal overnight."

Working quickly, they set up camp, fed and watered Storm and Silver and then settled down beside the fire they'd lit.

Soon Tom could hear Elenna's soft breathing as she slumbered. Sleep did not come so easily to him. Images of the Beasts he had fought on his

Quests in Tavania came back to him in a rush. They'd been ferocious, driven mad because the portals in Tavania's sky had ripped them from their true homes and dropped them into strange places. Tom felt sure that his battle against Krestor would be the fiercest yet. *But I will face him. And I will win.* Eventually, his eyelids grew heavy. The last thing Tom saw before falling asleep was a shooting star, arcing across the sky.

As dawn broke, Elenna stirred the embers of the fire and boiled up some of the jerky that she kept in Storm's saddlebag. She tossed in a little of their salt and pepper, and Tom inhaled the aroma.

"I'm ravenous!" he said, grabbing

a piece of meat and tearing into it
with his teeth. They ate in silence
until the last piece of food had gone.

Tom got to his feet and led Storm
round in a wide circle, while Elenna
put out the fire. He smiled as he saw
that Storm was putting weight on his
ankle. "The compress worked!"

As the sun climbed higher in the
sky, Tom and Elenna rode on towards
the castle, Silver racing beside them.
Drawing up to the head of the path

that led to the stronghold, they could see that the castle was damaged. Sections of wall had come away and lay in piles of rubble, one of the towers has been completely destroyed, and the solid iron gates hung off their hinges.

"What's happened?" Elenna asked. "Do you think the Beast has left the mountains and come into the castle?"

Tom frowned. "It's possible, although it could just as easily be Malvel's forces." He sat up straighter in the saddle. "We'll have to go inside and ask some questions." He snapped the reins and they trotted down the stone road that led to the castle.

He drew Storm to an abrupt halt as he spotted a young boy tending a herd of cattle outside the fort's gates.

We can ask him to tell us what

happened here, Tom thought eagerly.

Jumping off his horse, he strode up to the boy.

"Stop, right there," the boy barked. He lifted his staff threateningly. "Take one more step and I'll crack your skull open."

CHAPTER FOUR

WANTED!

"We mean you no harm," Tom said, raising his hands in a gesture of peace. "We just want to know what happened to the castle."

The boy looked uncertain, his hands loosening on the staff slightly. "Y-you're not here to steal my cattle?" he asked. "Because if you are, I won't give them up without a fight."

Elenna appeared at Tom's side. "We're not here to do anything like that, I promise."

She stepped towards him and held out her hand. "My name is Elenna and my friend here is Tom."

The boy wiped his palm on his rough trousers and cautiously held it out. "My name is Finn."

"Nice to meet you, Finn," Tom said, shaking his hand. "Can you tell us what happened to this castle?"

Finn shook his head and pointed to a stone cottage some distance away. "I was in there with my grandfather when the castle was attacked. I didn't see anything."

Tom frowned. They still didn't know whether it was Krestor or Malvel's forces that had nearly destroyed the castle. He stared at the gates. Elenna nodded once and Tom knew that she was thinking the same thing.

"Will you look after our animals while we investigate what happened to the castle?" Tom asked.

"We'll be able to move much more quickly that way," Elenna added.

Finn looked unsure. "I have to take care of my herd. You may not be raiders, but others could still be around."

"We'll make it worth your while," Tom insisted, reaching inside his jerkin for one of the gold coins he had found during his Quest against Amictus the Bug Queen.

Finn took the coin and bit the edge to check that it was real. "We have a deal." He knelt down and rubbed behind Silver's ears. "I'll look after

your animals." He glanced over at
Storm. "I've even got some hay
for my cattle, which your horse
can share."

Tom patted Storm's flank, pleased
that he was going to be well cared
for. Storm turned his head and
nuzzled his shoulder. Tom stroked
his horse's head and Elenna hugged
her wolf.

"See you soon, Finn. You have no idea how much you're helping," Tom told him.

Then he and Elenna strode through the castle's broken gates to see what they would find.

They found themselves in a stone courtyard. Market stalls lay smashed on the ground, and men and women bustled about trying to prop up

falling masonry and clearing the
dust and broken stones.

"It looks even worse inside,"
Elenna whispered.

"Ssh." Tom put a finger to his lips
as a faint, eerie wailing sound filled
the air. "Can you hear that?"

Elenna cocked her head to one
side. Her face paled. "They sound like
people in pain," she murmured.
"We've got to help."

They tracked the source of the
noise to a long building just off the
main courtyard. Peering through,
they saw a broken window and
an infirmary packed with rows of
makeshift beds, each one containing
an injured man.

The smell of unwashed bodies filled
their nostrils and Elenna pulled her
collar up over her nose. Some of the

men were groaning in pain, clutching at gashes and wounds. Others lay still – too still. Their faces were a sallow yellow, like candle wax.

They went to the door of the infirmary but an old woman blocked their way.

"We don't want your type 'ere," the old woman said. "You're trouble and I'm not having anything to do with you. I don't care how much gold is on offer!" Her eyes flickered to something over Tom shoulder's before she slammed the door of the infirmary shut.

Tom and Elenna whirled round to see a poster pasted to the wall. On it were crude drawings of a boy, a girl, a horse and a wolf.

It's us! Tom thought, amazed. *There's no mistaking our faces.*

The words under the sketch read:

WANTED!
For a reward of 1,000 gold pieces
By order of Malvel

"He's put a bounty on our heads," Elenna groaned. "Again! He did exactly the same thing when we were on our Quest to defeat Narga the Sea Monster. You'd think he'd get some new ideas!"

Tom put a hand on Elenna's arm as he noticed a movement out of the corner of his eye. "We have company," he murmured, looking round at the brawny men who had suddenly surrounded them. One in the group, a powerfully built man with several deep scars on his arms, stepped forward. His gaze was hostile.

"The soldiers who attacked the

castle put up that poster," the man growled. "Malvel's launching surprise raids on castles and homesteads, looking for YOU."

The man jabbed a finger into Tom's chest. "It's your fault the castle was attacked."

So it is Malvel's men who harmed these people, Tom thought.

Another burly man stepped forward. "We should hand these two over," he said to the scarred man. "At least that way we can claim the reward."

"Malvel is the enemy, not us," Tom said. "We're trying to defeat the Dark Wizard so that he can't attack the people of Tavania any more."

The man with the scars gave a snort before grabbing one of Tom's arms. His friend seized the other.

"Let go of him!" Elenna shouted. "He's trying to help you. Can't you see that?" She reached for her bow and arrows but another man swiftly grabbed her, gripping her so she couldn't use her weapons. Elenna shook her head in disgust. "Malvel won't give you a reward for catching us. He's a liar."

One of the men gave an evil smile. "You're right, maybe Malvel isn't the answer. Perhaps we should kill you instead." He took a knife from his belt. "Your deaths will be payment enough for all the lives that have been lost here."

CHAPTER FIVE

THE DEAL

A trickle of sweat ran down Tom's
spine. The man's eyes blazed with
anger, but Tom did not drop his own
defiant gaze.

"Wait, Arket, let's not be too hasty,"
said one of the men holding Tom.
"Let's take them to see Lord Osric.
He'll decide."

Tom and Elenna twisted in the grip
of their captors, but with so many

men holding them it was impossible to break free. They were dragged into the castle and through to a large room where tapestries of great and bloody battles hung on the walls. Tom could see gashes in the woven wall hangings where they had been damaged in the raid.

The air was knocked from Tom's lungs as he was hurled in front of a throne. Elenna landed with a thud beside him. Swords were held to their throats.

Tom looked up to see a trestle bed hidden in shadows just behind the regal, gilt chair. A young man lay on the bed groaning with pain, while an older man knelt beside him, clutching his hand.

"Lord Osric," the man with the scars said. "We have brought you the two people responsible for the destruction to our home."

The older man turned, his eyes red and swollen from crying. His long grey hair was lank and his shoulders

hunched over as he stood and walked towards them, his damson cloak swirling around him.

Tom shared a look with Elenna. His hand crept to the sword at his waist.

The coldness of steel pressed even more strongly against his throat. "Don't even think about it," a voice growled.

Lord Osric looked in disgust at Tom on the floor. "So, you would bring more fighting to this place? Even as my son lies dying in this bed?" Lord Osric's nostrils flared with anger. "Because of Malvel's desire to find you, my son Alric was wounded in the battle against his men. Amends must be made."

"No, Father!" Alric's weak voice came from the bed. "No more death."

"Lord Osric," the man with the

scars said, swiftly speaking over Alric. "Do we kill them or give them to Malvel?"

The lord paused for a moment and shook his head wearily. "My son is right, I want no blood on my hands. I will not kill them. Give the prisoners to Malvel and let's hope that the Dark Wizard leaves us in peace." Lord Osric turned from them. "Now go, I don't have much time left with my son."

Tom struggled to free himself as he was hauled up off the floor.

"Wait," Elenna cried out. "I can help your son."

Lord Osric whirled round to face her. "Many have tried to heal him," his voice cracked. "Nothing works."

"Let me try," Elenna begged. "And if I heal Alric, you must set us free."

Good thinking, Elenna! Tom thought.

Osric glanced back at his son. Tom could see how torn he was. "All right. We have an agreement. If you save my son's life I'll set you free."

The man who held a sword to Tom's throat did not move, but Elenna was allowed to cross over to the bed where Osric's son lay. She pulled back the covers and Tom could immediately see the cause of Alric's ailment. A deep gash slashed across the young man's thigh, and the wound was black and foul smelling.

"The sword that inflicted this wound was poisoned," Elenna said. She touched Alric's brow. "The poison is spreading into his blood but there is still time to stop it. Listen carefully. I'll need a cauldron of hot water, the bag of herbs from my quiver and some juniper berries."

A cauldron was set up above the great fireplace and a servant brought the juniper berries from the kitchen.

Come on, Elenna, Tom thought. *I know you can do it!* He had been allowed to get to his knees and now he craned his neck to watch what his friend would do next. Lord Osric peered over her shoulder while the man with the scars shook his head in disgust.

"A waste of time," Tom heard him mutter.

You don't know my friend, Tom thought.

Elenna swiftly made a broth with the ingredients and then carefully spooned it into Alric's mouth. She smeared some of the liquid onto his leg, then carefully wiped the sweat from his brow and rearranged the blankets over his body. After a while, the young man's laboured breathing

sounded looser. When Elenna peeled back a corner of the blanket, Tom could already see that the blackness in his leg was a little better.

Alric smiled at Elenna. "Thank you," he said, his voice hoarse. "You saved my life."

"Release the boy!" Lord Osric boomed, whirling around from his son's bed to face his men. He stood straight now, his face filled with joy. "He and his friend are heroes."

The man holding a sword to Tom's throat stepped away. Tom got to his feet, his limbs stiff. His hand went to the hilt of his sword and this time no one tried to stop him. But Tom wouldn't seek another fight here. Elenna came to stand by his side.

Lord Osric shook her hand. "How can I thank you?" he asked, looking from Elenna to Tom.

"Simple. Keep your promise and let us go free," Tom said.

"Of course. Anything else?" Lord Osric asked.

"Perhaps some information," Tom suggested. "We're searching for a

Beast. Have you heard of anything strange in these parts?"

Osric shook his head.

"Wait, I have." Alric sat up weakly in his bed. "I've heard rumours of something evil lurking in the mountains."

"Why are you looking for this Beast?" Lord Osric asked.

"I have a Quest," Tom replied simply.

Normally, he wouldn't tell the people of his own kingdom about his Quest against the Beasts. But here it was different... There was a chance that Tom's arrival in Tavania had torn open the portals, so it was down to him to put things right in the kingdom. Didn't the people have a right to know that angry Beasts were roaming?

"Then you must finish what you set out to do," Lord Osric murmured. He looked over at his men. "These two heroes are to have free passage through my lands. Make sure all my citizens know." His men nodded in agreement. "The best of luck, brave warriors."

"Thank you," Tom said. But he knew he'd need more than luck. A mighty Beast was waiting for him in the mountains. It was a Beast cast far from home. Krestor would be dangerous and deadly.

CHAPTER SIX

AN UNEXPECTED DISCOVERY

The afternoon sun was hot on the back of Tom's neck as he and Elenna rode up the mountainside path. The peaks of the mountains were black and shadowy against the sky. Dusty ridges of rocks surrounded them.

They'd collected Storm and Silver from Finn and waved goodbye to the cattle herder.

"Good luck," he'd told them with a smile. "Whatever it is you're doing."

"Oh, just trying to save the kingdom," Elenna had joked. Finn's eyes had widened for a moment, before he shook his head in disbelief and turned back to his cattle. Tom wondered if they'd see him again.

"Don't you think it's odd that Malvel had to organise raids to track us down?" Elenna asked, interrupting Tom's thoughts. "He's a wizard – why can't he just use his dark magic to find us?"

Tom smiled grimly. "Raiding that town had nothing to do with finding us," he replied. "It was just a good way of turning the people of Tavania into our enemies."

"And it almost worked." Elenna said, sounding glum.

A chill suddenly passed through Tom, despite the bright sunshine. He glanced about him; something didn't feel right. Everything looked so dead and he couldn't hear the crash and roll of gullies and streams, or the scuttle of wildlife; the mountain seemed completely lifeless.

Silver let out a yelp as he slipped on the pebbly mountain ground. With a whine, he sat down and licked his sore paw.

Tom halted Storm. "Look at how dry the ground is," he said. "It looks like it hasn't rained here for weeks."

"Do you think that it could have something to do with the portals affecting things in Tavania?" Elenna asked as she climbed down and checked Silver's paw.

"It could be," Tom replied,

dismounting. He glanced up at the portal swirling in the air above their heads. A Beast had fallen through there. Krestor might be watching them right now.

The dusty path ahead twisted and turned. Drooping plants bordered it and he could see the surface of the path breaking up because it was so dry.

"I think we'll need to walk rather than ride from here. The trail is getting really slippery. Storm could lose his footing at any moment."

Elenna ruffled Silver's fur, and Tom took Storm's bridle as they continued their climb. The path got narrower and soon they were very high up, panting for air. The clouds were so low that Tom felt like he could almost touch them. The portal hung over them like an angry, bleeding wound in the sky.

"Arghhh!"

Tom swivelled round to see Elenna teetering precariously on the edge of the mountainside path. She must have slipped; the dirt on the path was so dry and dusty it was crumbling at the edges!

He hurtled over and grabbed her collar, yanking her back. Elenna collided into him, sending them both sprawling to the ground.

"Are you all right?" Tom asked, feeling a bit winded as they got to their feet.

Elenna looked over her shoulder, her whole body shaking. "The path just gave way beneath me." She swallowed hard. "I thought I was going to fall. Thanks, Tom."

Tom looked further up the path and saw a skeleton bleached white by the sun, and a head crested with a pair of twisted horns.

"I think that must have been a mountain ram. There's a drought." Tom said. "It's killed all the wildlife." He looked up at the portal again. "I wonder if the Beast is to blame? The

sooner we send it back home,
the better."

They climbed higher still, looking
out for any sign of the Beast. Storm
whinnied as a shower of small rocks
tumbled beside them, revealing a
trickle of water oozing down the
rockface. Storm stepped forward,
eager to drink the water, but Tom
pulled him aside.

Smoke rose in a slim column from
the rocks. Tom could see the liquid
eating through the stones. They
fizzed and shrank away.

"It's acid!" Tom said.

Silver sniffed the air, whining in
agitation. Elenna knelt down and
held onto the ruff of his neck,
making sure that the wolf didn't go
anywhere near the deadly stream.
But he howled and backed away.

A larger pool of acid suddenly flooded the rock. There was a cracking sound and the rock face shattered. Tom and Elenna leapt to one side as a column of stones fell away. The pool of acid now became a torrent and it rushed down the mountainside, triggering other rock falls as it burnt through more stone.

"Where's the acid coming from?" Elenna whispered, her face twisted with worry.

Tom frowned. "The Beast doesn't belong in these mountains and neither does acid. Krestor has to be close by."

Silver suddenly lifted his head and sniffed the air. With a yelp, he pulled away from Elenna and bounded over some boulders.

"He might have caught the scent of

Krestor," Tom said, drawing his sword. It wasn't his Avantian sword – that was locked up in the palace dungeons after being taken from him by evil Malvel. But this one would have to do. "Stay here with Storm, Elenna."

His friend nodded and took hold of the stallion's bridle while Tom pursued Silver. His heart pounded in his ears as he scrambled up over a boulder and onto an outcrop. *Am I about to face Krestor?* he wondered.

He froze as he took in the scene before him. Silver had found something, but it wasn't a Beast.

The wolf was standing guard by a large nest woven from twigs and leaves tucked away in a nook of the cliff face. Tom stepped closer and saw that three eagle chicks were sitting in

the nest, their downy feathers
wafting in the cold breeze. They
were cheeping hungrily.

Tom went to the edge of the
outcrop and beckoned Elenna to join
him. She quickly tethered Storm to a
dead tree and climbed up to him.

Elenna gasped as she saw the little
chicks. "They're so young," she

murmured. "Where do you think their parents are?"

"They may have died in the drought," Tom replied. "Or that acid got to them."

Elenna made a clucking sound in her throat. "We have to take care of them," she said. "But we should be careful not to touch them, just in case their parents are around. We don't want them to reject the chicks because we've disturbed the nest."

"How do we take care of them?" Tom asked. "There's nothing around here for them to eat."

Elenna looked thoughtful, and then her eyes lit up. "We can use the last of the jerky from Storm's saddlebag!"

"Good idea." Tom ran back to his horse to get their water flask and their dried meat. Together he and

Elenna soaked the jerky, shredded it and dropped it into the nest. The chicks devoured the meat greedily, fighting each other for scraps. As soon as they'd gulped down the last bit, their little beaks opened in wide, red ovals demanding more. The cheeping was earsplitting.

Elenna looked at Tom. "They're still hungry and we've got nothing more to give them."

"We've got some water," Tom said, lifting his water flask.

He filled the empty jerky pouch with the liquid and Elenna rested it up against the edge of the nest, securing it with pebbles.

"That should be enough water for now," Elenna said. "Maybe we can check later and see if their parents have come back."

Tom was about to reply when the noisy chicks suddenly fell silent and cowered against the bottom of the nest. He felt the hairs on his arms stand up. "The chicks have sensed something," he told Elenna.

He whirled round, expecting to see the Beast. But there was nothing except a huge boulder covered in green moss. He scrambled onto it, pulling himself up with gritted teeth. Standing with legs braced, he looked around to see if he could spot Krestor in the surrounding area.

"Nothing," Tom said turning to face Elenna. "There's nothing out here—" He broke off as he saw Elenna's face.

She was pointing to the boulder. "Krestor is here," she whispered. "He's right...under...your feet!"

CHAPTER SEVEN

THE BEAST'S SECRET WEAPON

The ground shifted and surged upwards. With a yell, Tom leapt off what he had thought was a boulder and somersaulted through the air. Landing softly on the balls of his feet he turned, his weapon raised.

Tom swallowed hard, his sword-hand clammy. Krestor the Crushing Terror stood before him.

Their eyes locked. The battle was on.

"Elenna, cover me from behind!" Tom cried. "We'll need to fight this Beast together."

Elenna grasped her bow and took an arrow from her quiver before running over to join him. Silver followed closely at her heels, barking loudly and furiously.

Tom held out his sword, pointing it towards his opponent's throat. If Krestor wanted to attack, he would have to get past his blade first. The Beast stalked forward, pulling his enormous green body from the rocks

where he had been camouflaged. His head was large and bony, and spines sprung up and quivered along his back. He stood on broad webbed feet, which Tom could see were more suited to the ocean than the mountains. *This Beast is far from home*, he thought.

Krestor saw the determination in Tom's eyes. He opened his jaws in a cry of rage and showed rows of glinting, sharp teeth.

"Tom, I'm going to try and shoot him in the leg," Elenna yelled. "It will slow him dow—" But before Elenna could finish her words, Krestor swooped down and smashed his head on the ground like a club.

Elenna cried out as they both sprawled in the dust. Tom just about managed to hold onto his sword.

The Beast beat at the rocky path again, sending splinters of stone flying in all directions. Shards of rock sliced into Tom's skin like tiny daggers. Silver gave a pained yelp. "We've got to get to higher ground," Tom cried, as another splinter tore at his cheek.

A Beast who can use his head as a

weapon! Tom thought. *His skull must be as strong as iron!*

He and Elenna scrambled to their feet and ran towards a narrow ridge of rock that jutted out from the mountainside. Silver bounded after them. Tom was glad that Storm was tethered at a safe distance. The ground juddered beneath them as Krestor continued to slam his head onto the earth, but Tom and Elenna crouched low and kept their balance.

As they climbed up onto the rocky platform, Silver gave a howl of warning as a jet of clear, foul-smelling liquid hurtled past Tom's ear. It splashed onto part of the ridge and Elenna gasped as the rock cracked into pieces in front of them.

"It's acid, just like we saw before," Tom said turning to face the Beast.

"It must be Krestor's weapon."

The Beast gave another roar, and
a spray of acid shot out of the spines
on his back. Tom leapt in front of
Elenna and threw up his shield. The
acid splattered onto the wood and
Tom could smell smoke as it passed
straight through the timber and
landed on his arm. His skin blistered.

Tom gave a growl of pain. His shield fell from his grip as he dropped to the ground and curled into a ball. The agony of the burn made him want to faint. His eyes began to close but he fought against it. Elenna crouched over him in concern, while Silver jumped in front of Krestor and bared his teeth with a snarl.

Krestor roared back. His snake-like neck whipped out and wrapped

around the wolf, lifting him up.

"Leave my wolf alone!" Elenna shouted furiously. She took an arrow and shot it into the base of the Beast's neck. But Krestor swatted it away with one of his webbed claws as if it was no more than an annoying mosquito.

Elenna gave a cry of frustration and continued to shoot arrows, even though Krestor knocked them away

with ease. "I've run out of arrows," she told Tom desperately.

"It's all right," Tom said, gritting his teeth against the burning pain in his arm, and the wooziness that was still trying to overwhelm him. "I'm going to save Silver."

He stood, swaying for a moment, then shook his head and charged forward with his sword. With a cry, he hacked at the Beast's flank, swiping with deadly accuracy. But as he struck a final blow, Tom saw how his blade skidded off Krestor's hide.

It wasn't sharp enough! *I wish I had my proper sword*, Tom thought. Then he stood straighter. *No, I can't feel sorry for myself. I have a Beast to defeat.*

Thinking quickly, Tom took the hilt of the sword and smashed it into the Beast's side. He brought it down again and again with all his might. The Beast gave a snarl of fury and hurled Silver to the ground.

The spines on Krestor's back began to vibrate and more jets of acid shot from the quills hitting the mountainside above Tom's head.

"Tom! Watch out!" Elenna screamed, pointing upwards.

Krestor's acid rapidly ate through one of the mountain's overhanging ridges and Tom saw a shower of rock hurtling towards him.

He tumbled out of the way, holding up his battered shield to protect himself. The rock fall landed with a crash and a cloud of dust.

Tom coughed and looked around. The shattered stones had formed a tall wall that separated him from Elenna and Silver and put them out

of sight. Now it was just him and
the Beast on the jutting outcrop.

He was trapped. From the outcrop,
he could see Storm further down the
mountainside. His horse was trying to
pull away from the tree he'd been
tethered to. Tom knew his brave
stallion wanted to help him, but he
was glad that Storm was out of reach
of the Beast. The fight was now
between Tom and Krestor.

The Beast seemed to smile, his jaws
opening like an inky well. Krestor
smashed his head on the ground
once more, the tremors forcing
Tom backwards.

"Tom, are you all right?" Elenna
called. "I can't see you. I'm going to
climb over."

"No, stay there," Tom yelled back.
"Gather up your arrows."

Krestor fired out another stream of acid. Tom managed to dodge out of its way but the acid struck the end of his sword, making the tip of the blade burn away. *I might as well be unarmed*, Tom thought angrily. *Wait! I can do something else.*

He felt along his jewelled belt for the amber gem he'd won from Tusk the Mighty Mammoth – it would give him better fighting skills.

Krestor approached slowly, his webbed claws slipping on the rocky ground. Far from his watery home, he couldn't walk easily on the stony path. He lurched from side to side. Tom stood firm, ready to fight, even as the Beast's stinking, warm breath rolled over him. The Beast roared again and lifted his head, seeking a chance to deliver a deadly blow.

CHAPTER EIGHT

A FRIEND FROM ABOVE

Tom was holding his broken sword high, ready to meet Krestor's attack, when a dark blur descended from the sky. An eagle! The mighty bird landed on the Beast's head and pecked at his skull, its curved beak tearing at Krestor's green flesh. With a fierce caw, the eagle darted from side to side as Krestor swung at him.

Tom saw his chance to get off the narrow outcrop. Running for the wall of rocks that blocked him from Elenna, he pushed off the ground and jumped upwards. Grabbing a piece of jutting rock, he heaved himself up onto the wall. Elenna, Silver and Storm were below, and Tom saw that Elenna had gone to fetch his stallion. He watched as his friend reached for the last of her arrows on the ground.

"Hey, I'm up here," Tom called. Elenna looked up and smiled in relief as she saw him. Silver howled in delight and Storm gave a whinny of welcome.

Tom glanced up at the eagle. The feathers on the bird's right wing were burnt away, and its face was scarred, his beak damaged.

Yet still the eagle managed to dodge the Beast's snapping jaws to slash at him with its talons. But Tom could see that the eagle was getting tired. *I can't let him get hurt more than he already is.*

"What are you waiting for," Elenna called up to him. "Climb down!"

"I will," Tom replied. "But I have something to do first." He took his sword and brought it down against the wall to make a noisy crashing sound. Krestor's head snapped in his direction and the eagle took its chance to flap away to higher ground, exhausted.

Krestor's spines quivered and, in the blink of an eye, darts of acid jetted out from his spines and slicked the wall of rock that Tom was standing on. He felt the wall shift and crack. Then slowly it collapsed beneath him as acid ate through the rock. The rocks beneath his feet crumbled away and he leapt through the air landing beside Silver, Elenna and Storm.

"You're lucky," Elenna said. "You could have been trapped under those boulders."

"I'm fine," Tom reassured her, even as Elenna's words echoed in his head. *Trapped under those boulders*... "That's it!" he said aloud. "Swords and arrows don't work against this Beast. We've got to turn Krestor's acid on himself." He grinned. "We're going to imprison him under some rocks!"

There was a roar and Tom looked over to see the Beast pushing his way through the rubble of the collapsed wall.

He was coming for them!

They scrambled up the mountainside, taking advantage of Krestor's awkwardness over the rocky terrain to put some distance between them. Tom led the way, zigzagging across the mountain path to avoid Krestor's jets of acid, which streaked through the sky.

When they were high above the Beast, they urged Silver and Storm to stand behind a pile of boulders.

"Ready to put our plan into action?" Tom asked.

"Absolutely," Elenna replied. "Let's give Krestor a taste of his own medicine!"

Tom grinned. "Follow me."

They ran out to a ledge that hung over the Beast's head. Tom smashed his sword against the outcrop to get Krestor's attention.

"Come on," Tom called, pointing at his chest. "Come and get me!"

"And me!" Elenna cried, joining in with the taunting. It didn't matter if the Beast could understand what they were saying, as long as he understood he was being taunted.

Krestor reared up on his hind legs, roaring with fury. Tom could see pure rage in his enemy's eyes. Being far from his sea home had truly driven Krestor mad. The Beast's spines quivered violently, and a jet of acid shot up to where Tom and Elenna were standing. "Jump!" yelled Tom.

He and Elenna hurled themselves aside and the acid hit the ledge that they had been standing on only moments before. There was a hiss, then a crumbling sound as chunks of rock rained down onto Krestor, pinning him to the mountainside. He writhed, his mouth frothing with rage.

The Beast fired more acid, directing it at the rocks that pinned him down.

"Oh no," Elenna said. "The acid is going to eat through the rock. He'll escape!"

Tom shook his head. "It's all right, Elenna." He watched as the deadly liquid managed to eat through some of the rocks that covered Krestor. The Beast desperately tried to shove the

rocks away but the acid continued to burn and bubble, flowing towards him. Patches of Krestor's green skin immediately started to blister and turn red, as acid splashed onto the Beast's body. Krestor gave a roar of pain, his eyes rolling back in his mighty head, before he went limp.

Tom and Elenna climbed down towards the Beast, wearily circling him. Krestor stirred a little, but all the fight had gone out of him. His eyes closed and Tom could see one of the Beast's acid wounds getting worse.

"What do we do now?" Elenna asked.

Tom looked at Krestor and knew he had defeated the Beast.

"The Beast is at our mercy," he said softly. "He's been defeated and it's time for him to go back to where he belongs. We don't need to hurt him any further."

Tom crouched down beside Krestor and the great Beast put his snout into Tom's hand. All the fury had vanished from his eyes.

There was a crackle of lightning

and Krestor was snatched up into the air, his huge body flying through the sky and into the boiling red heart on the portal that slashed the sky.

Tom and Elenna shielded their eyes from the glare, glad to see Krestor transported to his rightful home. Then, with a final blinding flash, the portal closed like a trapdoor.

"He's gone," Tom said, sheathing his sword. "The mountains of Tavania are safe."

CHAPTER NINE

THE NEXT QUEST

A long object twisted and turned through the sky as the portal shrunk to the size of a coin and then disappeared. This part of Tavania's glassy skies was smooth once again.

Tom stretched his arm skywards and snatched the object out of the air. It was a magic wooden staff. He held it straight, driving it into the earth. It came up to his shoulder and was covered with intricate carvings:

a trailing snake and a pair of spreading falcon wings.

"It's another item belonging to Oradu!" Elenna said excitedly. "We already have two others!" As she said this, the Good Wizard's cloak and hat floated out of Storm's saddlebag, growing in size to hover before them.

Silver sniffed at the floating items suspiciously.

Tom felt the staff tug away from his hand and it joined the other suspended items. The air shimmered and the Good Wizard appeared in a ghostly form wearing the hat and cloak. His glowing fingers clasped his staff. "Congratulations, Tom and Elenna. You have completed another Quest successfully."

Tom felt a tingle of pride as he thought of all the Quests that he and

Elenna had undertaken. An image of
the Beast he had just battled jumped
into his head. It had been a hard
battle and his arm still stung from
where he had been burnt with acid,
but he did not blame Krestor. The
Beast had been driven mad because
he had been far from home.
Tom knew what it was like to
be homesick.

The burn on his arm suddenly felt
icy cold.

"Heal." The words came from
Oradu. The wizard was pointing his
staff at the burn and a tendril of
smoke left the staff's tip to wrap
around Tom's arm. After a moment
the smoke faded and Tom saw that
his acid burn was completely healed.

He touched his arm in wonder.
"Thank you."

The wizard dipped his head. "It's the least I can do."

"Oradu, you look stronger than you did last time," Elenna commented. "And healing Tom like that needs powerful magic."

Oradu nodded, his cloak billowing softly in the breeze. "With each Beast you defeat, and each magical item you recover from the portal, I become stronger and Malvel becomes weaker." The wizard's eyes twinkled. "I know someone else who is getting stronger, too." He used his staff to draw a circle in the air, which started to fill in with colour and movement.

Tom could tell that it was a vision of some kind, but it was covered in mist. Eventually the vapour settled and revealed some floating images. Tom felt a smile tug at his lips as he

saw Freya, his mother. She was
fencing with a soldier, her hair flying
behind her.

"She's training Dalaton!" Tom
whispered. He grinned to himself.
From the sweat on Dalaton's brow

and the strips of colour on his paunchy cheeks it was clear that Freya was working him hard to turn him into a true warrior.

"Yes, under Freya's tuition, Dalaton may one day be the Master of the Beasts in this kingdom," Oradu said.

The vision faded and Oradu's face became serious. "There are still other Quests to complete and the next Beast you must defeat is Madara. Be on your guard, for this Beast is a formidable enemy. The best of luck Tom and Elenna. Tavania is depending on you." These last words were an echo on the air as the Good Wizard disappeared.

Tom tucked his broken sword into his belt and turned to Elenna.

"Time to go?" she asked with a grin.

Tom nodded.

"Good, I won't be sad to see the back of this mountain." Elenna gave a sharp whistle and began to weave her way down the path, with Silver at her heels.

Tom smiled as he noticed that the dead-looking plants that lined the path already appeared much healthier. The dried out gullies and streams had started to flow with crystal clear water.

Tom grabbed Storms bridle and followed. They had another Beast to find and another Quest to complete – there was no time to waste. Malvel had to be defeated and taken from Tavania's throne as quickly as possible. The people of this land had suffered enough.

"Tom," Elenna suddenly called.

"Come and look at this."

Leading Storm, Tom caught up with his friend. She was standing some distance away from the nest they had found earlier that day. The chicks were cheeping excitedly – and being fed by the eagle who had saved Tom!

He was tearing strips of meat for the chicks from a rodent caught between his talons.

Now Tom was closer he could see that a few downy new feathers were replacing the burnt ones on the eagle's wing.

Tom smiled at Elenna. "The kingdom is healing itself," he said. "And while there's blood in my veins, I won't rest until Malvel is banished for good."

Here's a sneak preview of Tom's
next exciting adventure!

Meet

MADARA
THE MIDNIGHT
WARRIOR

Only Tom can save Tavania from the
rule of the Evil Wizard Malvel...

PROLOGUE

Jude grinned as he stole towards the cattle pen. He could hear the cows moving about nervously inside. He glanced up at the Tavanian night. Ripples of colour moved around a long dark slash in the sky. The patterns glowed with an eerie light.

"No wonder the cows are restless," he muttered. He looked away, concentrating on the task at hand.

Usually, the cattle pen's gate would be under constant guard. But Malvel had called all able-bodied men to join his army. Now, the countryside had emptied out nicely! Nicely if, like Jude, you were a thief.

"Come to Jude," he whispered, opening the gate. "Come and make me some easy money."

He slipped inside, smelling the animals all around him, hearing the thud of their hooves on the ground. The cows jostled against one another as he walked among them, running his hand over their flanks.

Finally, he slapped the haunch of a cow. "You'll do, my sturdy friend."

A moment later he had slipped a noose around the cow's neck and was leading it out of the herd.

He walked the cow out of the cattle pen and closed the gate. But as he began to lead his four-legged prize towards where he had tied up his horse, he stopped, his ears pricking at a strange sound. A low growl.

Then a second sounded out of the darkness, deep and resonant. He bit his lip and shivered. The cow snorted and rolled its eyes, fretfully pulling on the noose.

"Steady," Jude said, but his voice was trembling. He pulled the cow to his tethered horse, over by a tree. Quickly mounting, Jude tied the end of the noose rope around the saddle pommel. He spurred his horse into a gentle trot, pulling the cow with him.

"We've done well tonight, my friend," Jude said, patting his horse's neck. "Plenty of meat for the butcher. Why, we'll feed on the profits for—"

Another eerie growl stopped the words in his throat.

His horse faltered, tossing his mane nervously. The cow lowed and dragged back on the rope, the bell around its neck jingling. The sound was closer this time – much closer.

Follow this Quest to the end in
MADARA THE MIDNIGHT WARRIOR.

Win an exclusive
Beast Quest T-shirt and goody bag!

In every Beast Quest book the Beast Quest logo is hidden
in one of the pictures. Find the logos in books 37 to 42
and make a note of which pages they appear on. Write the
six page numbers on a postcard and send it in to us.
Each month we will draw one winner to receive
a Beast Quest T-shirt and goody bag.

THE BEAST QUEST COMPETITION:
THE LOST WORLD
Orchard Books
338 Euston Road, London NW1 3BH
Australian readers should email:
childrens.books@hachette.com.au

New Zealand readers should write to:
Beast Quest Competition
4 Whetu Place, Mairangi Bay, Auckland, NZ
or email: childrensbooks@hachette.co.nz

Only one entry per child.
Final draw: September 2011

You can also enter this competition
via the Beast Quest website: www.beastquest.co.uk

Join the Quest,
Join the Tribe

www.beastquest.co.uk

Have you checked out the Beast Quest website? It's the place to go for games, downloads, activities, sneak previews and lots of fun!

You can read all about your favourite beasts, download free screensavers and desktop wallpapers for your computer, and even challenge your friends to a Beast Tournament.

Sign up to the newsletter at www.beastquest.co.uk to receive exclusive extra content and the opportunity to enter special members-only competitions. We'll send you up-to-date info on all the Beast Quest books, including the next exciting series which features six brand-new Beasts!

☐ 1. Ferno the Fire Dragon
☐ 2. Sepron the Sea Serpent
☐ 3. Arcta the Mountain Giant
☐ 4. Tagus the Horse-Man
☐ 5. Nanook the Snow Monster
☐ 6. Epos the Flame Bird

Beast Quest:
The Golden Armour
☐ 7. Zepha the Monster Squid
☐ 8. Claw the Giant Monkey
☐ 9. Soltra the Stone Charmer
☐ 10. Vipero the Snake Man
☐ 11. Arachnid the King of Spiders
☐ 12. Trillion the Three-Headed Lion

Beast Quest:
The Dark Realm
☐ 13. Torgor the Minotaur
☐ 14. Skor the Winged Stallion
☐ 15. Narga the Sea Monster
☐ 16. Kaymon the Gorgon Hound
☐ 17. Tusk the Mighty Mammoth
☐ 18. Sting the Scorpion Man

Beast Quest:
The Amulet of Avantia
☐ 19. Nixa the Death Bringer
☐ 20. Equinus the Spirit Horse
☐ 21. Rashouk the Cave Troll
☐ 22. Luna the Moon Wolf
☐ 23. Blaze the Ice Dragon
☐ 24. Stealth the Ghost Panther

Beast Quest:
The Shade of Death
☐ 25. Krabb Master of the Sea
☐ 26. Hawkite Arrow of the Air
☐ 27. Rokk the Walking Mountain
☐ 28. Koldo the Arctic Warrior
☐ 29. Trema the Earth Lord
☐ 30. Amictus the Bug Queen

Beast Quest:
The World of Chaos
☐ 31. Komodo the Lizard King
☐ 32. Muro the Rat Monster
☐ 33. Fang the Bat Fiend
☐ 34. Murk the Swamp Man
☐ 35. Terra Curse of the Forest
☐ 36. Vespick the Wasp Queen

Special Bumper Editions
☐ Vedra & Krimon: Twin Beasts of Avantia
☐ Spiros the Ghost Phoenix
☐ Arax the Soul Stealer
☐ Kragos & Kildor: The Two-Headed Demon
☐ Creta the Winged Terror
☐ Mortaxe the Skeleton Warrior

All books priced at £4.99,
special bumper editions
priced at £5.99.

Orchard Books are available from all good bookshops, or
can be ordered from our website:
www.orchardbooks.co.uk,
or telephone 01235 827702, or fax 01235 8227703.

FREE COLLECTOR CARDS INSIDE!

Series 7: THE LOST WORLD
COLLECT THEM ALL!

Can Tom save the chaotic land of Tavania from dark
Wizard Malvel's evil plans?

978 1 40830 729 8

978 1 40830 730 4

978 1 40830 731 1

978 1 40830 732 8

978 1 40830 733 5

978 1 40830 734 2